Maritza

LEAD ♥
With Your
HEART

by Angela
Cervantes

D0089899

★ American Girl®

**FOR MY ABUELOS:
ESPERANZA AND ANDRÉS
—AC**

ABOUT THE AUTHOR

Angela Cervantes is the author of several children's novels, including *Gaby, Lost and Found* and *Lety Out Loud*, which was a Pura Belpré Honor Book. Angela's inspiration to write started during her childhood, when she loved to read but could never find books that reflected her Mexican American heritage and community. Today, Angela lives in Kansas with her family. When she's not writing, she obsesses over her favorite soccer teams and runs every chance she gets. Keep up with Angela at www.angelacervantes.com.

ABOUT THE ILLUSTRATOR

Caroline Garcia is a freelance illustrator based in São Paulo, Brazil. She graduated from the University of Advertising in 2016, and decided to become a full-time illustrator. She creates covers and book illustrations for children and teenagers. Caroline aims to inspire young people with the colorful worlds she creates.

ADVISERS FOR MARITZA'S STORY

Deanna Singh leads workshops on creating impactful social and personal change. She founded Flying Elephant, a consulting firm to help women and people of color become social entrepreneurs. She has written four children's books about racism, including *A Smart Girl's Guide: Race & Inclusion*.

Deborah Rivas-Drake is a professor of psychology and education at the University of Michigan, where she studies how teens navigate issues of race, ethnicity, racism, and xenophobia. She wrote the award-winning book *Below the Surface: Talking with Teens about Race, Ethnicity, and Identity*.

Yasmine Mabene is a student at Stanford University. A teen activist, she is the California State Director of March for Our Lives, a youth organization working to prevent gun violence, and the social media coordinator of Earth Uprising, an international youth-led organization that works to fight climate change through education.

M. Lucero Ortiz is a human rights attorney with a focus on family and immigration law. Prior to joining Kids in Need of Defense as the Deputy Director for KIND Mexico, she represented migrant families and unaccompanied children before the Departments of Homeland Security and Justice.

Hi! We're Maritza, Makena, and Evette. We want to live in a world where everyone is treated fairly and with respect. We believe that if we work together, we can build a future that works for all of us. Best of all, we don't need to wait until we grow up to make a difference—we can do it right now! Together, we have the power to create the kind of world we want: *a world by us.*

ABOUT ME

Name: Maritza Ochoa
My first name is pronounced mah-REET-zah, My friends call me Itza
Hometown: Washington, DC
Birthday: April 10
School: DC Bilingual Middle School

THIS *Princess* WEARS CLEATS

MOM
Erika

DAD
Enrique

BROTHER
Javier

ME & SUERTE
Our playful pug

BOLIVIA

HOME
Washington, DC

MEXICO

Abuelo Joaquim   Abuela Silvana

Abuelo Julias

Abuela Nora

TICKET   TICKET   SHOWCASE   SOCCER SHOWCASE   SHOWCASE

This is my aunt (Tía) Mari. I was named after her. She gave me this journal and added special quotes to inspire me.

Tía Mari

Favorite foods: Too many to list! This week's favorite: elotes (eh–LOH–tehs). Corn on the cob with LOTS of queso fresco.

SOCCER

Makena and Evette are my newest friends. They want to make a better world just like I do —right now!

Mis amigas from school. Sierra is my oldest friend and dances ballet folklórico. Violeta loves soccer just as much as I do.

Violeta
Sierra

DC BILINGUAL MIDDLE SCHOOL

Evette   Makena

Friends

FESTIVAL

GIRLS PLAY, TOO

Chapter 1

The aroma of grilled corn on the cob wafted through the festival. My stomach growled loudly. My best friend, Sierra, shook her head and laughed as we waited for our order from the MexiExpress food truck.

"Here you go, Itza," said Mrs. Mendez. I grabbed the hot-off-the-grill corn, called an elote, from her. She had prepared it just the way I liked: with mayonnaise, cotija cheese, a squeeze of lime, and Tajín, a tangy lime and chile pepper seasoning.

"Gracias, Mrs. Mendez!"

It was October in Washington, DC, which meant the Columbia Heights neighborhood was celebrating Hispanic Heritage Month with a fiesta. DC's official fiesta is held near the National Mall, but my family prefers this smaller fiesta smack in the middle of Columbia Heights.

Outside, a large stage was set up for bands and dance groups. A children's soccer match was about to begin in an empty grassy lot, and all around us were food trucks and stands serving tasty treats from all over Latin America.

"You make us all proud," Mrs. Mendez said, pointing at

the shiny first-place medal draped around my neck. "Keep it up!"

"Thank you!" I managed to say through a mouthful of juicy elote. Running always makes me hungry. And since I had just won first place in the youth 5K race, I could have eaten a dozen elotes.

"The band is about to begin!" Sierra squealed, stuffing a bunch of napkins in my hand. She hooked elbows with me and pulled me from the food truck toward the stage. "My dance group is next!"

Sierra has been my best friend since we were in diapers. We both live in the Capitol Hill neighborhood of Washington, DC, and attend DC Bilingual Middle School. We're both seventh-graders, and we're both Mexican American. I'm also Bolivian American on my mom's side. Still, that's not why we're best friends. We're best friends because we both enjoy the same things: festivals, food trucks, bookstores, baby goat videos, pugs, dancing, and, more importantly, we love soccer. Except this year, after nearly seven years of game-winning goals, heartbreaking losses, scraped knees, and a few bloody noses, Sierra quit our school team, the DC Jaguars. She made it clear that soccer wasn't *that* important to her anymore, which made me feel like I wasn't that important either.

When I told my parents how I felt, Dad said I had to

support Sierra's passion for Mexican ballet folklórico the same way she supports me. In fact, at this morning's race, she had joined my family near the finish line, holding a big pink sign that said, "Itza Ochoa's #1 Fan!" In those last few seconds of the race, when I could hear my classmate Raheem huffing and puffing close behind me, Sierra's pink sign was like a power boost!

Still hooked at the elbows, Sierra and I zigzagged through the crowd toward the stage. As we inched forward, several people called out my name with a felicidades or congratulations for winning today's youth race.

"You know, you're practically a celebrity now, Itza," Sierra said. "The young girls look up to you. You have to start dressing the part."

I stopped in my tracks, unhooking my elbow with hers.

"What's wrong with my style?" I said playfully. I did a slow twirl showing off my usual look of leggings, track jacket, sporty fanny pack, and my "I Run DC" T-shirt. "I think I look very sporty-chic!"

Sierra was definitely more dressed up than I was, but that's because she was dancing tonight. She had silk ribbons woven into her long braids. Large gold hoops dangled from her ears, and she wore a turquoise traditional Mexican blouse with embroidered blue and purple flowers over a denim skirt.

"Stop being a goof," Sierra said. "After the race you should have changed into the beautiful blouse I brought you from Guanajuato, you know? Instead of a T-shirt."

"You're right," I agreed. The blouse she gave me was identical to the turquoise embroidered blouse that she was wearing, but in coral. I relinked elbows with her. "I love that blouse, but Raheem has been texting me about a rematch, and I can't run in a blouse."

"Tell that to Lorena Ramírez and the Tarahumara women of Chihuahua, Mexico. They run marathons in traditional blouses, skirts, and huaraches on their feet."

"Huaraches!" I exclaimed in disbelief. There's no way I could run in flat leather sandals. "Do they win?"

"Yes!" Sierra said incredulously. "They win ultramarathons—they're amazing. I can't believe you haven't heard of them." I made a mental note to look up Tarahumara runners. If they were Mexican athletes, I should definitely know about them.

"I promise I'll wear the blouse for something super important." Sierra seemed satisfied with my answer and linked arms with me again.

When we finally got to the performance area, I spotted my parents and my abuelos in the front row.

"VIP seating! Vamos! Let's go!" I exclaimed. As we took our seats, the band came onstage. They played music from Veracruz, Mexico, called son jorocho. At the very first joyful thrum of the guitars, the crowd jumped to its feet. Sierra and I danced around.

"Javier is up soon," my mom said, nudging me excitedly. On cue, my big brother walked out onto the stage dressed in all white with a red sash around his waist and a straw hat. The crowd roared as he took his place on a wooden platform and began stomping out a fast-paced dance step in sync with the band. It was like playing a drum with your feet! My parents pulled out their phones to record him.

"Someday, I want to do zapateado," Sierra shouted to me over the music. "Do you think I could do it?"

"You've always been good with your feet," I said, sending her a sly reminder that she used to be really good at soccer. If she caught my reference, she didn't show it.

The entire crowd danced. It was times like these that I truly loved Columbia Heights. Because my mom grew up here and my abuelos still live here, I feel like I have two neighborhoods: Capitol Hill and Columbia Heights. Sort of how I feel being Mexican American and Bolivian American. I belong to both. Can you belong to two communities? Two cultures? I say, yes! Definitely.

Just then, I noticed a small girl in a soccer jersey and shorts weaving through the crowd toward me. It was Yesenia from the soccer team that my father coached. I helped him with the team every weekend. They named themselves the DC Azules for the color blue that is in the flags of all the countries the team members are from: Honduras, Guatemala, El Salvador, and the United States. As Yesenia moved closer, I noticed that she looked sad. Before she could reach me, I rushed to her.

"Everything okay?" I asked as Yesenia threw her arms around my waist.

"I've been looking all over for you and your dad," Yesenia said, taking my hand. "The children's soccer game is about to start and they won't let girls play. And if we can't play, we can't win any prizes," she said, touching my first-place medal. "And the prizes son buenísimos—so great!"

Sierra joined in. "What's going on?" she asked.

"For some reason, they're not letting the girls play in the soccer match," I explained.

"What?" Sierra said with disgust. "Who's the organizer?"

"This year it's Mr. Ramos," Yesenia answered. Sierra and I exchanged a knowing look. Sierra and I used to play on a coed team and whenever we came up against Mr. Ramos's all-boy team, he'd criticize his players for losing to a team of girls. As if losing to girls was the worst possible insult! I didn't know Mr. Ramos very well, but what I did know was that he had some very old-fashioned beliefs. Someone had to challenge him on this! For a second I thought about telling my dad, but I didn't want to pull him away from Javi's performance.

"Hold my elote," I said to Sierra.

"With pleasure!" Sierra said with raised eyebrows. "I'd go with you, but I have to get ready for my performance."

"I got this," I said confidently. "Could you let my parents know where I am?" Sierra gave me a thumbs-up.

"Please be back for my performance, okay?" she said, taking a huge bite of the elote. My stomach growled.

"Definitely!" I yelled back.

SOCCER DREAMS
Chapter 2

As Yesenia and I reached the soccer field, I looked around for Mr. Ramos.

"Itza!" someone called out. It was Violeta Moreno. She jogged over to me.

I was so happy to see her! She's a seventh-grader like me and new to our school. She plays on our soccer team as a forward, which means she's always moving to the net and ready to strike. I should have known that I'd find her near a soccer game. From what I knew of her so far, she lived and breathed soccer.

We greeted each other with our soccer team's elbow-to-elbow tap.

"Did you hear? Mr. Ramos isn't letting the girls play," Violeta said with exasperation.

"Did he say why?" I asked.

"He says the girls will get hurt," Violeta said, rolling her eyes. "But the boys could get hurt, too, and they're still playing."

"Not cool," I said.

"My prima, my little cousin Mia, wants to play." Violeta

gestured to a little girl dressed in an El Salvador national team soccer jersey and shorts. Her dark-brown hair was tied up into a high knot. She looked like a miniature Violeta, and it made me smile.

"Mia is your cousin? I know her," Yesenia said.

Violeta smiled. "Why don't you go over there and warm up with her," she answered. Yesenia ran off toward Violeta's cousin and quickly joined in dribbling the ball around.

"We can't let them down," I said. "Let me talk to Mr. Ramos."

"He's over there," Violeta pointed. "I'll go with you."

Mr. Ramos was surrounded by a bunch of boys warming up to play. I recognized some of them from my grandparents' neighborhood.

"Hola, Mr. Ramos," I said in the most cheerful voice I could muster. He looked up from his clipboard and smiled wide.

"Maritza Ochoa!" he exclaimed with a toothy grin. "It's so good to see you! Look, muchachos," Mr. Ramos called the boys' attention. "She's a winning runner." He gestured at my medal. Suddenly, I was swarmed by a dozen boys hurling questions.

"How fast did you run to win the medal?"

"Is it made from real gold?"

"Can we take a selfie with it?"

I quieted the boys and turned back to Mr. Ramos.

"Mr. Ramos, I heard that the girls are not being allowed to play. I thought it must be some sort of misunderstanding because girls have always played in the festival's games."

"No misunderstanding, Maritza. I made the change for the girls' safety."

"Safety? But..." I felt my face get hot. I couldn't let myself get upset. I took a deep breath. It was like playing soccer when I'm being marked by two players. I had to find another path to the net.

"If they get hurt, I get blamed," Mr. Ramos explained.

"Oh, I see…" My mind raced. Mr. Ramos was afraid of being blamed. I totally got that. Soccer could be tough. I've had my share of bruised ribs and bloody noses. Still, Mr. Ramos seemed to think that only the girls would get hurt. It didn't make sense. "Keeping all the kids safe is a huge responsibility," I started. "But everyone knows your reputation, Mr. Ramos. You don't put up with roughness."

Mr. Ramos looked down at his clipboard. Was he even paying attention?

Violeta stepped closer to take a shot at it. "That's why the community admires you. You teach the kids to play fair. If a few players get out of hand, you'll red-card them and they'll lose any chance to win a prize."

"At school, the girls always play with the boys," I said. "The girls are tougher than you think."

Mr. Ramos nodded, and I felt a surge of optimism that maybe he was coming around to our side. I passed a wink to Violeta and she raised her eyebrows, a hopeful look on her face.

I thought of one last point to make. "Please let the girls play, Mr. Ramos. The next Messi could be in this game today, but also the next Marta or Megan could be here."

Mr. Ramos quietly leafed through the papers on his clipboard. After a few seconds, he looked up at me. "The next Marta and Megan, eh?"

I nodded. "Definitely."

And I truly meant it. Why couldn't the next soccer champion come from Columbia Heights?

"Okay, muchachas! Let's play!" Mr. Ramos shouted to the girls. Behind us, the girls and boys cheered. I high-fived a bunch of them.

"Gracias! Thank you!" Mia and Yesenia shouted back at Violeta and me as they ran toward the field.

"That was cool," Violeta said, giving me a fist bump. "You sounded like a real coach."

"Thanks. My dad coaches a team here in Columbia Heights. I help him out."

"Like an assistant coach?"

"I guess," I said with a shrug. "And don't laugh, but my dream is to play for the US Women's National Team and then be the team's first Latina coach."

"Why would I laugh at that? That's an awesome goal!"

We both laughed at the pun.

"Truth is, my dream is to play for the US women's team, too, but..." Violeta's smile faded, and she turned her gaze toward the soccer field as if her dream were out there being kicked around.

"But what?" I asked. "If you work hard, you can achieve your dream. That's what this country is all about."

Violeta looked down at her shoes. "I hope you're right,"

she said with a tinge of sadness that I wasn't used to hearing from her.

Suddenly, a loud crescendo of trumpets blared from the stage.

"Sierra's performance!" I shrieked. "I have to go. You want to come?"

"Thanks, but I should stay with my prima."

"Of course. See you at school!"

We parted with fist bumps. I ran fast. My already exhausted legs stiffened, but I pushed through. I reached the front of the stage just as all the dancers in colorful traditional dresses and black and silver charro suits glided across the stage for the grand finale of the jarabe tapatío. My mom and dad looked over at me with quizzical faces that asked, *Where have you been?* I mouthed an apology. I had missed the entire dance performance! How was that possible? I waved to Sierra. Her red-lipped smile disappeared, and she scowled. Was she mad at me? Definitely.

A BETTER LIFE
Chapter 3

"I can't believe you missed the whole performance!" Sierra complained. She and the entire dance troupe were gathered around El Sabor de Honduras food truck. It served yummy baleadas, which are large flour tortillas smothered with beans and cheese and drizzled with Honduran sour cream.

"Yeah, what happened to you, Itza?" Javier asked, handing me a warm baleada. "Sierra and I danced La Bamba and she forgot how to tie the ribbon." Sierra pushed him playfully.

"I slipped a little," she laughed. "I was nervous!" They continued to joke about the performance. A pang of regret surged through me for missing it. La Bamba is known as the wedding dance. The two dancers tie a ribbon with their feet and hold up the ribbon at the end. It was Sierra's first time, and I had missed it.

"I'm sorry. I wish I could have seen it. I tried to be quick, but then I bumped into Violeta and we started talking."

"I was counting on you to be there, Itza," Sierra said. She scowled at me for the second time that evening. "So, instead of watching me dance, you were talking to Violeta?"

"It wasn't on purpose," I said.

Sierra took a huge bite of the baleada as if to avoid saying something rude. I gazed around the festival and sighed. Everything was winding down. A group of men were folding up chairs and taking down the stage. It felt like Sierra was closing up on me, too.

Just then, I heard Raheem's voice. He was the last person I wanted to see. Surely, he didn't want to race now.

"What's up, mi gente? My people!" Raheem shouted. He dangled his second-place running medal around so everyone could see. "Ready to settle who is the fastest once and for all?" He smiled and wriggled his dark eyebrows at me.

"Maritza already proved it this morning," Sierra said, defending me, which made me smile.

Trying to avoid him, I got up to order a bottle of water from the food truck. On the counter, I noticed a large donation jar with a photocopied picture of a family taped to it. I picked up the jar and examined the photo more closely. "Are they sick?" I asked the food truck owner.

"The father has been detained by immigration. We're collecting donations to help pay for his legal fees."

The whole group quieted. Everyone knew what being detained meant: The father had been arrested by immigration officials because he didn't have citizenship papers to show them. He could be sent away to his home country and separated from his family here in the United States at any moment. There wasn't much money in the jar. Clearly, it wouldn't be enough to help with lawyers.

"That's horrible," Raheem said what all of us were thinking. The picture was of a mom and dad and two girls sitting on a park bench. Both girls looked like they were about six or seven years old. In fact, one of the little girls looked familiar, but I couldn't place her. The description said that the parents were from El Salvador. It also said that the father was an invaluable member of his church and community and came here for a better life.

I unzipped my fanny pack, scooped out what was left of my prize money, and put it in the jar. It wasn't enough

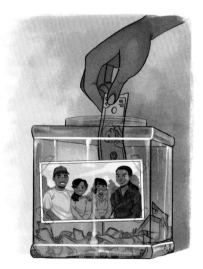

for a lawyer, maybe thirty dollars, but the jar felt fuller.

"Okay, that makes up for missing my performance," Sierra said, throwing her arm around my shoulders.

"Really?" I was relieved. Sierra was my best friend, and I didn't want her mad at me or thinking that I didn't support her dancing.

"Yes, now please go and race Raheem so he'll be quiet."

Raheem was doing quick high knees. "A race to the light post and back, Itza," he said. He signaled to a post at the end of the block.

"Hold my baleada," I said to Sierra, handing the half-eaten folded tortilla to her. I pulled my hair into a high ponytail, tightened my shoelaces, and removed my first-place medal from around my neck. Suddenly, it hit me where I'd seen that little girl from the photo on the donation jar. It was Violeta's little cousin. It was Mia!

As if I'd just tripped, I felt like I was falling, helpless.

"Are you okay, Itza?" Raheem asked.

I stood frozen. Could it be true? Was Violeta's uncle detained?

AMIGAS
Chapter 4

Javier and I spent the night at our abuelos' apartment in
Columbia Heights. We did this whenever we were in the
neighborhood for an event or Javi's dance practice. When
I woke up, I had the urge to talk to my tía Mari about
Violeta. Tía Mari was my dad's older sister. It was an honor
to be named Maritza after her. She had lived in Los Angeles
and had been a nurse. She fought to save lives as a nurse
and she spoke out for causes she cared about. She believed
that everyone's voice is important and that we need to speak
up for those who can't. I believe that, too.

We used to have video calls every Sunday night. During
those chats, she'd tell me about her work and her cat, Canela,
who loves to eat ants. I'd tell her about school and my pug,
Suerte, who loves to chew up my soccer socks. But all of that
stopped when she became sick with cancer.

Before she passed away, I received a beautiful journal
from her in the mail. Inside, she had written inspirational
quotes from famous women athletes and leaders. On a note
enclosed with the journal, she had written that I should add
more inspirational quotes to the journal, because keeping a

positive attitude was important when life becomes hard. I had to admit, it was hard to be positive during that time.

I cradled the journal close to my chest and went to the kitchen. From a small speaker, my abuela's favorite singer, Mercedes Sosa, crooned a slow, melodic song called "Gracias a la Vida," which meant "thank you to life." My abuela hummed along as she and abuelo prepared breakfast. I took a seat at the kitchen table and opened my journal to a blank page. I used a purple pen, which was the closest color to violet I had, and wrote.

> If you were here, Tía Mari, I would tell you about my friend Violeta. Together, we convinced Mr. Ramos to let the girls play in the soccer game. It was awesome. But now I'm worried. I found out that Violeta's uncle has been detained by immigration. She doesn't know that I know. I'm not sure if I should ask her about it at school tomorrow. What would you do?
> I wish so much I could hear your voice.

I put the pen down; it was suddenly too hard to write.

"You're so quiet, I barely noticed you were here," Abuela said, pulling a tray of spicy meat-filled salteñas, Bolivian meat pies, out of the oven. She put the tray down on the stove and gave me a kiss on my head. "¿Todo bien? All good?"

"I miss Tía Mari."

"You're still writing to her in your journal, mija?" my abuela asked. I nodded. "That's good. She'd be very proud of you winning the race."

I took in a deep breath. "I miss talking to her," I said.

Javier joined me at the table. "I do, too," he said with a nod. "I bet she would have loved that you gave away all your prize money yesterday."

"What'd you do, mija?" Abuelo asked.

"I donated it to a family whose father has been detained by immigration."

"Ay, those donation jars for him are everywhere," Abuela said. "It's muy triste. So sad because he came to America for a better life and was working toward his citizenship. ¡Qué feo!" Abuela placed a plate of salteñas in front of me. "Such an awful thing! His name is Andrés. He has two US-born children. He worked as a cook at the hospital all through the pandemic."

"He was an essential worker, and this is how he's treated?" said my abuelo pouring himself a cup of coffee. "Shame on us."

"We have to pray for him," my abuela said.

"He'll need more than prayers," Abuelo grunted between sips of coffee.

I stared down at the salteñas, thinking of what my abuelo said. Prayers weren't enough, but sometimes prayers are all you have. Was there something more I could do?

"Well, eat up because we're going to Riverfront Community Center today," Abuela announced. "Your mom will meet us there to take you back home. There's a new Bolivian artist featured as part of the knitting exhibit. I'm excited to see her work."

My abuela, an immigrant from Bolivia, cofounded the Bolivian American Cultural Association in DC. They organize events to celebrate Bolivian culture. And her shop, Silvana's Capitol Hill Tailors, is one of DC's best. Her clients are some of the city's most powerful political leaders. She even fitted a dress for one of our First Ladies! Now that dress hangs on display at the Smithsonian.

"Abuelo, are you going with us?" I asked, already knowing the answer.

"No way! Knitting is boring. I have soccer to watch," Abuelo said, barely ducking in time as Abuela threw a wadded-up napkin at him.

"¡Ay, viejo! Old man! You're horrible!" she laughed.

I had to admit, my abuelos always cheered me up.

Riverfront Community Center in the Anacostia neighborhood is amazing. The best part? There is a soccer field behind it! Over the summer, our middle school used it for practice. Every time I go, the center is bustling with activity. There's a lounge with study tables, colorful couches, and a water station perfect for refilling my water bottle.

Mom was waiting for us inside the exhibit in front of an art piece made of knitted finger puppets. The finger puppets were positioned like they were participating in a march. The title of the piece was *Tu lucha es mi lucha*, which means "your fight is my fight."

"Maritza!" said two familiar voices. I looked over to see my newest friends, Makena and Evette, smiling at me. Makena was wearing the coolest sequin butterfly on her shirt. Evie was wearing fantastic platform shoes. They both had awesome style. I rushed over to give them hugs.

"It's so good to see you, chicas!" I said. Mom and Javier said hello, and I quickly introduced my friends to my abuela.

"Abuela, this is Makena and Evette," I said. "We worked together to clean up part of the Anacostia River. Evette had the idea to turn the tires that were polluting the river into beautiful flower planters. We sold them to make money for the food pantry here at the community center."

"Very impressive!" Abuela said. "Such talented girls." We all stood up a little straighter when we heard Abuela's compliment.

Evie took a closer look at the puppet exhibit. "This artist is originally from Bolivia. Isn't that where your family is from, Maritza?" she asked.

"My mom's side is from Bolivia," I said with a nod to Mom and Abuela. "My dad's side is from Mexico. I've visited Bolivia once, and we bought a bunch of these finger puppets."

"Very cool," Makena said.

"How about a selfie for our World by Us page?"
I asked. "The puppets want to make a better world just like
we do!"

We had created our own social change page to spread the
word about causes we care about. We called it World by Us
because we want to make a better world, starting right now.
We'd already made a difference with our river cleanup and
fundraising with upcycled tire planters, and we weren't
going to stop there.

Makena quickly snapped a shot of us in front of the finger puppets. "I'll caption it, *Your fight is my fight*. How's that?"

"Love it!" Evie and I said at the same time.

I pulled out my phone and snapped a picture of the title of the artwork, *Tu lucha es mi lucha*. Not only would I add it to my journal, but I planned to share it with Violeta.

"Do you have time to hang out for a little while?" Makena asked me. "Evette and I are here for another half hour."

"Mom? Could I?" I asked.

"Sure, I'm going to take a little more time enjoying this art exhibit with Abuela," Mom replied.

"Good," said Javier. "I want to talk with the center director to see if I can set up a performance for our ballet folklórico group."

"Let's go outside," I said to Makena and Evette. "I want to show you chicas some soccer moves."

"Cool!" Evette and Makena replied together.

We checked out a few soccer balls from the gym and headed out to the field. It was a perfect fall day—fresh, crisp air and a bright blue sky.

"Okay, here's a trick for you," I said. I set my soccer ball on the ground and squeezed it between my feet. Then I jumped and tossed the ball into the air with my feet. The ball went as high as my waist, and I used my knee to bump it into the air higher. I finished with a head bump before catching the ball in my hands. "Now you try!"

Makena and Evette burst into giggles.

"Are you kidding me?" Makena asked.

"Okay, here goes," said Evette.

I took out my phone, and my friends hammed it up for the camera, losing their balance and bumping into each other. Soccer balls bounced everywhere! We chased them around and then fell into a heap on the grass, laughing until we couldn't laugh anymore.

"You could start a new online trend—Silly Soccer Shots!" Makena said.

"It'll go viral," agreed Evette. "Look out, baby goats."

"Hey, don't mess with my baby goats," I joked. "Will I see you at my soccer game on Saturday?"

"Only if you do this trick in the middle of the game," Makena replied.

"We wouldn't miss it," Evette promised.

DIFFERENT OPINIONS
Chapter 5

At school, Sierra and I met at her locker as usual and walked to our current events class together. Once we took our seats, Violeta walked in with Ainsley Marks, our soccer team captain. Raheem was also in our class, and he showed up in a Barcelona soccer jersey, which was one of my favorite teams.

"Today we will learn about DREAMers, people who immigrated to the US from other countries when they were children," our teacher, Mr. Bernstein, announced from the front of the classroom. He was dressed in his usual blue jeans and a cardigan sweater over a concert

T-shirt. "I've sent all of you the link to our first article," he said. "Please read it and be ready to discuss."

I pulled out my tablet and started reading. It was an article about a medical student from South Korea who was brought to the United States as a child. His whole life he thought he was a US citizen. It wasn't until he applied for college that he realized his family's secret—they weren't citizens. Now, like all the DREAMers, he was waiting for Congress to act and grant him citizenship.

"Itza?" Mr. Bernstein called on me as he perched on the edge of his desk. "What did you think of the article?"

"It makes me sad for the guy because if he's not given full citizenship, he could be deported to a country he doesn't even know."

"How many of you think he should be granted full citizenship?" Mr. Bernstein asked. Most of the kids raised their hands, but a few didn't. "Why or why not?"

Josh raised his hand and Mr. Bernstein called on him. "I don't think so," said Josh. "He's here illegally. The law is the law."

Ainsley raised her hand. "But the US is the only home he has known."

Peyton's hand shot up. "He's exactly the kind of immigrant we should allow to stay in the country," she said. Violeta's face crumpled as if what Peyton had said was hurtful. Most of the class started commenting in agreement. I wasn't so sure I agreed with it, though. Did Peyton think that someone like Violeta's uncle didn't deserve to stay in the United States?

Before I could form my question, Raheem spoke up. "Peyton, are you saying that the only way an immigrant should be allowed to stay in this country is if they're a straight A student and in medical school? I know a bunch of US citizens in this class who wouldn't live up to that." A few of Raheem's friends laughed. "Seriously," Raheem continued in a voice more thoughtful than I expected. "My family is made up of immigrants from Ethiopia and Honduras. Some of them never went to college, because they never had the opportunity. Still, they worked and started their own businesses. They're living proof of the American dream."

Mr. Bernstein was nodding his head excitedly. Obviously, he was enjoying the exchange.

"I might have misspoken..." Peyton's voice softened. "Now that I hear what you have to say, there are lots of ways immigrant people contribute to society, and they're all important."

Violeta sat up a bit straighter in her chair.

"People have different views about immigrants and immigration." Mr. Bernstein nodded toward Josh. "Any additional thoughts to share, now that you've listened to other opinions from your classmates?"

Josh looked at Peyton, Raheem, and Sierra. "I hear what you say, but it's important that we respect the laws of our country, too. But maybe..." Josh paused to put together his thoughts, "maybe some of those laws could be changed one day."

"At the fiesta this past weekend, we heard about a family whose father was detained by immigration," Raheem said. "They were raising money for the dad's legal fees. If he gets released, maybe that could help change things for someone else."

I glanced over at Violeta. Her eyes darted toward the door, like she wanted to run out. I was worried that the discussion had upset her.

"Itza donated all of her prize money to help them," Sierra added. I shrugged bashfully when the whole class clapped. Violeta shot me a glance and smiled.

As soon as class ended, Violeta rushed out.

If the class discussion had upset her, Violeta showed no sign of it during pre-practice stretches. Still, I wanted her to know that I was on her side no matter what.

"That discussion in current events was kind of intense. What did you think?" I asked her.

Violeta shrugged. "Everyone has their opinions about immigrants, but until they've walked in their shoes, most people can't understand."

"Do you think there is a way we can help people to understand?" I asked.

Violeta stopped mid-stretch and frowned. "I don't think so."

Her response stunned me. I didn't want Violeta to lose hope or give up on the idea that people's opinions could change, or that hearts and minds could open.

We finished our stretches, and Ainsley, our team captain, started announcements. "I'd like to remind everyone that attendance counts. Unexcused absences will mean you could be benched. Please commit yourself to being here. Also, the Soccer Showcase is coming up. How many of you are signed up?" A bunch of hands went up, including mine and Violeta's. We were excited about the chance to be chosen for a club team! "Well, no matter what happens, our school team is still a team," Ainsley said. "Now, let's go, DC Jaguars!"

Everyone clapped and then jogged over to the field for a scrimmage. I was just about to run off when I noticed

Violeta hanging back with a serious-looking Ainsley.

"She's worried about our school team," Violeta explained when I came over.

"I've heard of other school teams falling apart after the Soccer Showcase," Ainsley said. "It's bad enough we lost Sierra this year to folklórico dancing. She was our best defender. The DC Jaguars can't afford to lose anyone else."

"I don't plan to quit if I get chosen for a club," I said.

"I don't either," Violeta said. "Playing for two teams would be awesome."

"You say that now, but the club schedule is super demanding," Ainsley countered.

I had an idea to cheer up Ainsley. I grabbed my journal from my backpack. "This was a gift from my tía Mari."

"The one who passed away?" Ainsley asked in a sad voice. I nodded.

"Lo siento," Violeta said, taking my hand and giving it a gentle squeeze.

"Thank you," I said. "She bought me this journal and filled it with inspirational words. When I'm upset, I read them." I opened the journal to a random page, landing on the perfect quote. "Here's one!" I said excitedly. "It's from tennis champion Serena Williams: 'I am lucky that whatever fear I have inside me, my desire to win is always stronger.'"

Ainsley smiled. "That's a good one," she agreed. "And I do feel better."

"Yay!" I clapped. "We will keep this team strong no matter what. Remember, we're young. No one expects us to be leaders, so we must expect it from ourselves."

Ainsley and Violeta exchanged an incredulous look.

"Whoa!" Ainsley said, throwing her hands up. "Is *that* quote in your book?"

I shook my head. "No, it just came to me right now. Why?"

Violeta grabbed my journal and the attached pen. "I'm writing it down," she said, busily scrawling on a blank page. "By Itza Ochoa, soccer player, and ..."

"Amiga," Ainsley completed, pulling us into a hug.

MORE THAN PRAYERS

Chapter 6

The next day, I rushed downstairs for breakfast before school. Suerte, our honey-colored pug, became excited and started chasing me. I think he thought I was heading for a morning run without him.

"Sorry, Suerte. Mom will take you for a nice walk. I have to go to school." I gave him a kiss on his sweet pug face. We had adopted Suerte, which is Spanish for "luck," from a rescue shelter shortly after Tía Mari was diagnosed with cancer. It was a very sad time in our house, and Suerte brought us so much joy and comfort that *we* felt lucky to have found *him*.

Dad put a plate of pancakes in front of me. "So, we have a busy week," he announced. "I have a big trial at work, and Mom will be putting in long hours for the future National Museum of the American Latino!" My dad announced the name in a dramatic fashion that made us all laugh. My mom rolled her eyes and took a bite of pancake. I was so proud of my mom being part of the team planning the national Latino museum.

"You got this, Mom!" I said, and gave her a fist bump.

"On Saturday, Itza and I have a DC Azules game, and then she has an afternoon match with an undefeated team. Yikes!" My dad continued, "Your abuelos will be there, but I can't be. I have to make sure Javi makes his dance performances."

"Hispanic Heritage Month!" Javier said with a big cheesy grin. "Everyone wants the Mexican hat dance this time of year."

"And don't forget the Soccer Showcase is coming up," I reminded everyone.

"It's going to be awesome," Dad said. He heads the showcase planning committee. "I've secured Riverfront's soccer field, and I've booked DJ Sol for the after-party."

"DJ Sol!" I squealed. I listened to him on a local radio station. He played all the latest Latin hits. I couldn't wait to trade my soccer cleats for some dancing shoes!

"Maybe you can use some of your prize money to buy a dress for the after-party," my mom said.

"One little problem," I said. "My prize moolah is gone."

"What? How?" Mom asked.

"At the fiesta, they were collecting donations for a man who's been detained by immigration," I said. "I donated it all."

"That was generous," my mom said.

"There's more," I said softly. "The man is Violeta's uncle."

"The new player on your team?" Dad asked.

I nodded. "She doesn't know that I know. I can tell she doesn't want to talk about it. I'm really worried about her."

"You have to pray for her," Mom said.

"Grandpa says prayers aren't enough," Javi said. Mom shook her head and chuckled.

"I want to help," I blurted out. "I'm just not sure how."

"Well, use our city as your inspiration," my mom said.

"We live in one of the most influential cities in the world. The National Museum of the American Latino would never have happened if a group of people hadn't organized to make it a reality. You're at the heart of where change happens."

I thought of the famous DC landmarks I grew up with, like the Lincoln Memorial, where Martin Luther King Jr. gave his "I Have a Dream" speech in 1963, or the National Mall, where people have marched for so many important causes. There was incredible history here, and yet...so much more history to be made.

"I want to do something that will open people's hearts. Are we seriously okay with families being separated or immigration officers picking up our neighbors?"

My mom looked over at my dad and they smiled. "You know who she sounds like?" Mom said.

"My sister," Dad said softly and tugged at the Virgen de Guadalupe medallion he kept around his neck. It was a gift from Tía Mari.

"I know your abuelo says prayers aren't enough," Mom said, "but let's say one anyway." We held hands and closed our eyes.

"Dear Virgen de Guadalupe, thank you for this beautiful day," Dad began. "Give our children the tenacity to accomplish their goals and to always give back and help others. Amen."

"And one little favor," I added. "Please tell Tía Mari we love her always."

Maybe I should have felt sad after a prayer like that, but instead I felt more eager to help Violeta. I had to talk to her. Together, we could come up with a plan to help her family.

"Way to go, Mia!" Violeta and I cheered from the sidelines as Mia darted past two of her opponents. She dribbled fast to the net and shot hard. The ball sailed into the net.

GOAL!

"Goal!" I screamed. Suerte, who I had dressed in a pug-sized light blue soccer jersey for the game, barked and did a little jump on his hind legs. Dad and I had taught him to do a special jump whenever someone yelled "Goal!" It was too cute.

Honestly, being outside on a crisp autumn morning cheering on the DC Azules was just what I needed. School had been busy, filled with a ton of homework this past week. Today would be busy, too, but fun! After our soccer match, I had promised Sierra I'd go shopping with her. I had hoped to invite Violeta, but Sierra shut that idea down so fast. She wanted time for just me and her.

The referee whistled, ending the game. The DC Azules won! Mia came running up to Violeta super excited. Suerte congratulated Mia with sloppy kisses, and she giggled. Mia and Suerte ran off to play a game of doggie tag.

"I'm so glad you brought Mia today," I said to Violeta. "Did you teach her how to play?"

"Her dad, my uncle Andrés, taught her," Violeta

said. "He also taught me." It was the first time Violeta had brought up her uncle, and I wondered if now was a good time to talk.

"I haven't seen him at the games," I said.

She nodded, but she looked uncomfortable. "Both of Mia's parents work long hours. I help out when I can."

I wanted Violeta to trust me with the truth, but I could see she wasn't ready to share it.

"I should take Mia home now," Violeta said.

"Okay, I'll see you at our game later. It'll be a tough one," I said.

"I'm ready!" Violeta said, doing a quick jog in place. We hugged good-bye. Dad and I watched Violeta and Mia walk away.

"She's the friend you told us about, right?" Dad asked once they were down the street.

"Yep," I answered.

"Be patient, Itza. She probably doesn't know who to trust."

I nodded. "But she can trust me."

Dad put his arm around my shoulder. "Think about how she must be feeling. She doesn't know what else might happen to her family, and they may not all be protected with citizenship. Before your abuelos became citizens, they feared so many things—like being late on rent or making

40

a mistake at work. Before your abuela had her own tailor shop, her old boss used to make her work late hours. If she objected, he threatened to have her deported."

I gasped. I hadn't heard that story.

"Luckily, your abuelos kept focused on getting their citizenship, and now they don't have to live in the shadows anymore."

I let my dad's words sink in. Hope filled me up like when my legs are tired, but I see the finish line.

"There is hope then," I said, feeling suddenly optimistic for Violeta and her family.

My dad nodded. "What does Violeta need most from you to find that hope?" he asked.

"She needs me to be her friend," I replied. And as soon as I said those words, I felt them in my heart.

Later that afternoon, my abuelos took me to the Riverfront sports field for my soccer match. As my abuelos took their seats in the bleachers, I ran inside the center to refill my water bottle. My phone pinged. It was a text from Violeta.

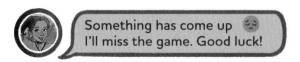

Something has come up 😔
I'll miss the game. Good luck!

Everything ok? 😮

Violeta didn't respond. I had just seen her two hours ago, and she said she was ready to play! Where could she be?

Just then, Evie and Makena walked in. They could see I was upset.

"What's wrong, Itza?" Evie asked, putting her arm around me. I was so worried for Violeta that I couldn't help letting a few tears slip down my cheeks.

Makena led us to a quiet table. "Are you worried about your game?"

"Yes and no," I said. "I'm worried because one of my teammates backed out at the last minute. She didn't give any reason and I'm afraid our coach will bench her. She's really good, and ..."

"And?" Evie asked.

I knew I could trust Evette and Makena with anything. "And her family has been going through a really tough time. Her uncle has been detained by immigration. They don't know if they'll ever see him again."

"Oh no!" Makena said, her eyes filled with compassion.

"Families belong together," Evie said. "Remember how you encouraged me to bring my grandmas together? Maybe you can help your friend figure this out, like you helped me."

"We'll help in any way we can," Makena said. "Your fight is my fight, right?"

"Tu lucha es mi lucha," I said as they pulled me in for a hug. "Gracias, chicas. You're the best."

Their words helped steady me. And as my tía Mari always said, I had to stay positive. Not just for me, but for Violeta, too.

Just then Ainsley rushed up to me. "Where is Violeta?" she grumbled. "I hope she gets here soon, or Coach will bench her."

I really didn't know what Violeta's excuse was, but I chose to believe that something miraculous had happened ... like Violeta's uncle was released, and the family wanted to be together. It was possible, right? I let that hopeful thought carry me through the game.

GOALS

Chapter 7

We won . . . barely. I scored in the final minute of the game. When the ball hit the net, my teammates tackled me with hugs. My abuelos and Makena and Evette jumped around and cheered from the bleachers.

As soon as the game ended, I messaged Violeta. I kept the text upbeat even though I was seriously worried.

 ¡Ganamos! We won! :) Are you ok?

No response.

"¡Que golazo! What an amazing goal, Itza!" my abuela squealed, pulling me into an embrace.

Makena and Evette danced around me and chanted, "Maritza's gonna defeat-cha!"

They pulled me in for one last hug before they had to leave.

"Text us about Violeta!" Makena whispered in my ear. I gave her a thumbs-up.

"I hope everything's okay," Evette added.

"Thanks so much, chicas," I said as they turned to go.

Abuelo grabbed my sports bag and slung it over his shoulder. "Who's hungry? Before the game I passed a church not far from our apartment setting up for a fundraiser," Abuelo explained. "They are selling pupusas!"

I was starving as usual, and pupusas—grilled Salvadoran flatbreads made from corn and stuffed with beans, meat, and cheese—sounded yummy.

"Since we're heading to your neighborhood to eat, maybe I could check on my friend Violeta? She didn't show up to play and I'm worried."

"Claro," my abuela said. "Of course."

We walked to the green line to catch the Metro to Columbia Heights. When we reached the church, we followed a group of people into a large dining hall, where tables were set up and there was a steady line of folks ordering food.

Suddenly, a woman stopped in front of us.

"DC Bilingual Middle School," she said, recognizing the school colors and logo on my jersey. "My daughter goes there. Her name is Violeta Moreno. I'm Gloria." I smiled and nodded, happy to meet Violeta's mom.

"Violeta's my friend," I said. "I'm Maritza. And these are my abuelos."

Violeta's mom and my abuelos exchanged greetings in Spanish.

"She'll be happy to see you!" Gloria gushed.

"Violeta is here?" I said with surprise.

She pointed to some tables across the room, where several people were packing up to-go orders.

"I know she missed the game," Violeta's mom said. "I told her to go, but she saw the crowd here and insisted on staying at the church to help. This is a fundraiser for her uncle. You understand, right?"

"Yes, of course," I stammered. My abuelos nodded, letting me know it was okay to go talk to Violeta. I looked around at all the people gathered. Did everyone know Violeta's uncle? Were these his neighbors? Coworkers? Friends? There were so many people.

I spotted Violeta still dressed in her soccer jersey. She looked shocked to see me but still managed a friendly smile.

"Itza!" she exclaimed. "How did you know I was here?"

"I didn't," I said. "My abuelos wanted pupusas after the game."

"I got your text that we won," Violeta said. "I'm sorry I missed the game, but I couldn't leave my mom and aunt with all this work."

"I get that, but you missed practice the other day and now today's game. Ainsley says Coach Smith is ready to bench you."

Violeta looked pained. "If I tell them what's really

going on," she said softly, "they won't understand. Just like in class."

"I disagree, Violeta," I said firmly. "In soccer, if we see something wrong, we call it out so it can be fixed. I see something wrong, and I want to help."

Violeta stepped back, stunned by my words. She gestured toward a table at the back of the dining hall. "Let's talk over there."

We sat down and Violeta finally trusted me with her truth.

"I wanted to tell you, but I wasn't sure if I could," Violeta said. I nodded so she knew I was listening. "My uncle is working toward citizenship," she whispered. "But it takes a long time and is very expensive. He's lived here for ten years with no problems, and then he was picked up at work by immigration. Now we're trying to raise money to get a lawyer for him."

"I'm so sorry," I said.

"It's been hard for everyone. I missed practice because my aunt had an appointment with my uncle's boss, and she needed help with translation. She had to go during the afternoon, while the girls were in school. Everyone else was at work, so there was no one who could help her except me. Everything has been a mess."

I took a deep breath. When immigration took Violeta's

uncle, it was like they'd taken the family to the edge of a cliff. And Violeta was trying her best to keep them from falling off.

"Aren't there organizations that can help?" I asked.

"Yeah, they're helping my aunt with her apartment. She can't pay rent on her own. Plus, every cent is being used for a private lawyer focused on the case."

"How much will that cost?"

"Thousands," she answered with a shake of her head. "You know in class when Sierra said you donated your race money? I wanted to thank you. That was so kind. I felt like telling you everything right then, but I was afraid."

"Everything?" I asked.

"Tío Andrés came here to work and send money back to El Salvador when my abuela became sick."

"I'm so sorry, Violeta," I said.

"When she died, he sent for our whole family. Including me, Itza."

Wait a minute, I thought. *Violeta is telling me she wasn't born in this country. Maybe she isn't a citizen either.*

"My mom and I arrived when I was very young, with only the clothes on our backs," she said.

"It must have been so scary," I said gently, not knowing what else to say. Violeta was already someone I considered kind and unstoppable, but now I knew she was also brave.

"My uncle Andrés is like a father to me." She peered up at me, and a tear dripped down her face. "You've lost your aunt. You know how it is to lose someone so close."

"We couldn't travel to Los Angeles to be with my tía Mari because of the pandemic," I said. "In my aunt's case, not being able to see her one last time was a matter of public health. But in your case, someone made a policy—a decision that meant someone had been taken from your family."

"It feels so heartless," Violeta said.

"I know sometimes it feels that way, but I believe America is better than that," I replied. I stretched my hands out across the table to grab hers. "Tu lucha es mi lucha," I said. "I will lead with my heart and find a way to help your family."

"How?"

"Remember that quote you wrote down in my journal?"

Violeta sat up straight and squinted at me like she was reading some hidden text in my eyes. "We're young ..." she said. "No one expects us to be leaders."

I smiled at her. "So we must expect it of ourselves."

I decided to stay with Violeta for the afternoon. I should have left to meet Sierra for our shopping trip, but I just couldn't. And I couldn't tell Sierra the reason—Violeta's truth was safe with me. I took a deep breath and made a video call to Sierra.

After two rings, she answered, looking very annoyed. "Where are you?"

"I'm sorry, Sierra, but I'm in Columbia Heights with Violeta and I won't be able to go shopping today."

"What?" I could feel her frustration through the screen.

"Look, if you don't want to be my bestie anymore because I left soccer, then you should just say it. I can find another best friend."

Her words stung me. I wasn't doing a good job apologizing or explaining. "But I don't want you to have another best friend. *We're* best friends," I stammered.

"It doesn't feel like it."

"I'm sorry. I'll make it up to you. Maybe we can

go shopping tomorrow?" I suggested.

"Forget it," Sierra said, hanging up on me.

I was stunned. In all the years I'd known Sierra, she had never hung up on me. I called back, but she didn't answer.

"Everything okay?" Violeta asked when I came back to the table.

I shrugged. "Sierra's disappointed."

My abuelos joined us at the table. Violeta opened up easily about her fears to my abuelos. They told her they knew what it was like to be here in the United States as an immigrant and struggle for a better life. They told her not to lose hope. Together, we brainstormed ideas to help Violeta's family. We needed to make people aware and be inspired enough to want to take action and make change.

"In the English Premier Soccer League the players took a knee before every game to show their opposition to racial discrimination," my abuelo said.

"That's right," I said.

"It makes me proud to see the game of soccer taking a stand like that," he continued.

Violeta and I looked at each other as if we were reading each other's minds.

"What if we made a presentation at our next game?" Violeta said, and then frowned. "Except no one shows up but family. We need a huge audience."

"The Soccer Showcase!" I exclaimed.

Violeta's mouth dropped open. "No, we couldn't! Could we?"

"Hundreds of people show up for it. My dad's organizing it, and he can help."

Violeta smiled wide. "Let's do it!"

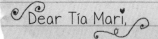 Dear Tía Mari,

If you were here, I'd tell you how I scored a game-winning **GOAL**, but that wasn't the best part of my day. The best part was that Violeta told me about her tío Andrés, and shared her own story. She's so incredibly brave. We've formed a plan to help her family, but it may mean that we have to disrupt the Soccer Showcase. The worst part of my day? Sierra is upset with me. I'm not sure she wants to be my best friend anymore, but I hope after Monday's current events class, she'll understand everything, because I want her to support our friend Violeta and her family.

GET INTO FORMATION

Chapter 8

On Sunday, I called Makena and Evette to fill them in on the plan.

"That's an awesome idea, Maritza!" Makena said.

"What a way to make a statement, and such an important one," Evette added.

"Let's use our World by Us page to get the word out," suggested Makena.

"Of course," I said, "why didn't I think of that?"

"What are friends for?" said Makena.

"If this isn't a World by Us event, I don't know what is!" Evette said.

This would be our biggest World by Us event yet. My chicas were all in and totally had my back.

The next day at school, Violeta and I sat down with Ainsley and let her know why Violeta had missed the game, and about our plan to help her family. Ainsley was completely supportive—and said she would convince the coach to give Violeta another chance!

Now we needed Mr. Bernstein. We found him in the library and told him about the special presentation we wanted to make to everyone. He agreed on the spot.

When class started, Mr. Bernstein told everyone he was letting Violeta and me take control. Sierra's face twisted in confusion, but she also looked interested. She hadn't spoken to me all day. I wasn't used to the silent treatment from her.

I started by bringing up a photograph on the board at the front of the classroom. It was the same photo from the donation jar. "Hi everyone! I want you to look at this image and tell me what you see."

Raheem was the first to raise his hand. "It's a family," he said. "They look like they're at a park."

I nodded. "Anything else?"

"They're smiling," Peyton added. "They're happy. I wonder who was taking the photo, because sometimes it's hard to get small kids to smile. I have two little brothers, and in every picture they frown or make goofy faces. Drives my parents nuts!"

I laughed with the rest of the class. "Cool. Any other thoughts?"

"They look like they could be Latinx? You know, Hispanic. Is that okay to say?" Josh said from the back of the room.

"Yes, that's totally okay. The reason I'm showing you this image is because last week Raheem mentioned that we

learned about a man who had been detained by immigration officers." Sierra's head snapped up and she sat forward in her seat. "Well, this is the man and his family."

Gasps filled the classroom.

"His name is Andrés and he's from El Salvador. At the age of eighteen, he left El Salvador. His family desperately needed money to pay for his mother's medical care. He couldn't make that kind of money in El Salvador no matter how hard he worked. He felt he had no choice but to come to the United States and work. Now, I'll pass the floor to Violeta."

Violeta walked up to the front of the classroom. "Settling here in DC, Andrés worked as a cook at a hospital. He joined a local Catholic church, fell in love, married, and now has two children named Mia and Graciela." Violeta stopped. She clicked the remote to return to the image of the whole family. "Peyton asked who took the photo. It was me. They're my familia, my family." Violeta spoke firmly. "This photo shows a happy family, but now his girls cry for him every day. His wife can barely make ends meet. My tío Andrés means so much to our family. We love him and we need him home."

The classroom was silent.

I snuck a look at Sierra. She mouthed the words *I'm sorry.*

Violeta said, "I'll turn it over to Itza for final thoughts."

Just then, Sierra led the whole class in a burst of applause. I took a deep breath to deliver a final point to my classmates.

"We don't want to just *talk* about injustice," I began. "We want to *do* something about it. What if I told you that our class has the power to help Violeta's family? Would you do it? Raise your hand."

"Count me in!" Raheem shouted.

"Me, too!" Ainsley said.

More hands and shouts of support followed.

"¡Sí se puede! Yes we can!" Sierra shouted. Then she smiled at me in a way that said she understood everything now.

Together, Ainsley and I had a video call with the other players participating in the Soccer Showcase to pitch our idea. Some of them worried that the presentation might hurt their chances to be selected for a team, but I had a great response. I found a quote in my journal by one of my favorite women soccer players, Megan Rapinoe, and read it to them.

I feel like it's actually everybody's responsibility to use whatever platform they have to do good in the world, basically, and to try to make our society better, whether you're an accountant or an activist or an athlete or whatever it is.

By the end of our chat, the whole team was excited to participate. Every day, my classmates updated me on influential people they had invited to the event.

"Itza!" Peyton stopped me at my locker. "My mom is a TV producer for the evening news. She's bringing a camera crew to the showcase."

"Thank you, Peyton!"

I had asked my abuela to invite what she called her "bigwig" clients. She wasn't so sure about contacting her customers about a cause they may or may not support, though. I'd have to do a little convincing. If they knew how important it was to bring this family back together again, I bet most of them would want to help.

Sierra took the lead in organizing some kids in our class to create social justice signs for the event. Violeta and I contacted our favorite food trucks and asked them to come to the showcase and donate some of their proceeds to Mr. Moreno's legal fees. They all agreed!

That night, I got a group text from Evette and Makena.

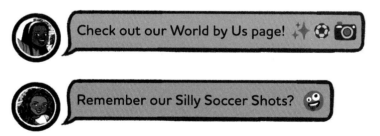

Check out our World by Us page! ✨ ⚽ 📷

Remember our Silly Soccer Shots? 😜

GET INTO FORMATION

I clicked on one video after another. Several players from my school's soccer team had made videos of themselves doing soccer tricks. Then they invited everyone to the Soccer Showcase. Makena and Evie were brilliant.

We would definitely be ready for the big day.

That Friday before the Soccer Showcase, Violeta and Sierra slept over at my house.

"So, is everything ready for tomorrow?" Javier asked as we finished dinner.

"I've scheduled time in the program for your presentation, and I have the audio equipment you need," Dad said.

"Thank you for helping us out, Mr. Ochoa," Violeta said.

My dad smiled at her. "My pleasure, Violeta. The whole family is very proud of you girls."

"Super proud!" Mom said, entering the dining room. She held a large photo album in her arms. She kissed each of us on the top of the head. "I found the photo album you wanted."

"Oh yeah!" I said excitedly, reaching for the album.

Sierra had told Violeta that I looked like my aunt, and now Violeta wanted to see pictures.

We moved to my bedroom and spread comforters and pillows on the floor and went through the photo album. It was full of pictures of my dad and his sister, Mari, as children and all through college.

SOCCER SHOWCASE!
Chapter 9

The next day, Violeta and I along with forty other girls were warming up on the field of the Riverfront sports complex. I kept an eye on the sidelines, where Sierra and Mr. Bernstein were getting kids organized. Every so often, Sierra would flash a thumbs-up to let me know that everything was going okay.

I looked toward the stands. My parents were already in their seats with Sierra's and Violeta's families. Mia held a soccer ball on her lap like she was ready to jump in if we needed a substitute. My abuelos were there, too. They sat next to another couple that I didn't recognize. The two couples chatted and laughed. My abuela had agreed to invite her bigwig clients, but I had no idea who they were.

Just then, we were called to line up for our scrimmage bibs. Violeta got a purple

bib. Ainsley and I both received blue bibs. We'd be playing against Violeta.

"Different teams," Violeta winked.

"But always united," I countered.

Sierra came rushing over as the DJ started to play a catchy dance tune. "DJ Sol is going to livestream our presentation. Turns out his parents are immigrants from Colombia. He's down with what we're doing!"

"Wow," I said. "I'm getting nervous."

"Don't worry. We wanted a crowd, and this is a huge crowd," Sierra answered. "The rest is up to you and Violeta." She gave me a fist bump.

"Itza!" I heard my name being shouted from the bleachers. I looked up, and it was Makena and Evie. They held up a sign that said, "Tu lucha es mi lucha!"

I blew them a kiss. I was so happy to see them.

Suddenly, the music stopped. DJ Sol introduced my dad and the entire Soccer Showcase planning committee. Sierra rushed over to the soccer players and got them in formation to hold up their signs spelling out our message.

As planned, my dad started calling out each player's name in the order we gave him. Each player kept her poster board lowered as she ran out to the field. Violeta and I joined my dad at the center of the field once all the players were lined up.

"Let's hear it for the Soccer Showcase!" my dad yelled into the microphone. The crowd cheered. "Before we begin, we have a special message from the players." Dad passed the microphone to me.

"Hi everyone! I'm Maritza Ochoa from DC Bilingual," I started. "All of us are united in our love for soccer, but we are also united in another cause that we want to share with you."

I blew a whistle. Each player lifted her sign over her head. Together, the signs spelled out "Families Belong Together." Silence fell over the crowd.

"Soccer has taught me many things, but most important it has taught me to be a team player and to be vocal if I see something wrong. This past week, I saw something wrong and I want to bring it to everyone's attention.

"The uncle of one of our teammates has been detained by immigration officials. His name is Andrés Moreno, and he lives in the community of Columbia Heights with his wife and two children. Mr. Moreno is a father, husband, and beloved member of his community and church. His family needs our help."

Violeta stepped up next. As she began to speak, Mia came running from the bleachers. As Mia took Violeta's hand and stood next to her holding her soccer ball, a low *Awww* rose from the crowd.

"My name is Violeta. I'm a forward for DC Bilingual. Andrés Moreno is my uncle. And this is Mia, my little cousin who loves soccer as much as I do. We both learned to play soccer from my uncle, her dad. My uncle Andrés always taught me to work hard to achieve a better life in this country. And that's what my family is trying to do every day. I'm not giving up hope that Mia will grow up with her papa and number one fan."

As Violeta spoke her last words, the crowd started cheering. Violeta handed the microphone back to me as everyone quieted.

I asked our current events class to stand up. "Today, we hope you'll help Mr. Moreno's family with their legal expenses. My classmates are happy to collect donations, and the food trucks are donating half their profits today,

too. More importantly," I continued, "we hope that you'll open your hearts and raise your voices for Andrés Moreno. To return him home to his family, we need everyone to speak up. Families belong together! Thank you!"

The referee blew her whistle to clear the field, and just like that, it was over. Violeta gave me a big smile and thumbs-up.

After the showcase, we made our way into the community center for a quick change of clothes. I put on the beautiful Mexican blouse Sierra had given me. I hoped Sierra would like the surprise.

"You were amazing, Itza!" Makena called when I came

out of the bathroom. She and Evie were sitting at one of the tables in the lounge, snacking on quesadillas from the MexiExpress food truck.

"We knew you could do it!" Evie exclaimed, giving me a high five.

"And I love that blouse," Makena added. We took a selfie, and Makena said she'd upload it to our World by Us page along with some other pics she'd taken at the presentation. I didn't know how much money we'd raised, but judging by the number of likes our page was getting, this event was a big success.

Just then, I felt a tap on my shoulder. "We'd like to interview you," a woman said. A camera crew stood behind her.

"Of course!" I said. An interview would be excellent coverage for our cause. Mr. Bernstein, Sierra, and our whole current events class gathered around me.

The reporter positioned me in front of my classmates. "Ready?"

I nodded. The camera started rolling.

"Tell me, what inspired you to make a stand today?" the reporter asked.

My heart pounded as I put every emotion I'd felt since learning about Violeta's uncle into words. "We've been discussing immigration in current events, and we wanted to make people aware of what is happening in our city. Mr. Andrés Moreno was detained by immigration authorities and we're asking that he be returned to his family."

I thought back to what Josh had said in our class discussion and added, "We're also asking our lawmakers to have compassion for immigrant families, so that no more families have to experience what the Morenos have gone through."

The reporter motioned to the camera operator to stop. "You'll be on the evening news. Great job!"

Sierra gave my arm a gentle yank. "You're wearing the blouse I bought you," she said, grinning.

I did a little twirl. "I told you I'd wear it for something super important."

Dear Tía Mari,

If you were here, I know we'd stay up talking all night about what happened at the Soccer Showcase. If you were here, you would have seen me stand up for Violeta and her family, and how incredibly brave Violeta was. You would have heard the crowd cheer and watched my interview for TV! If you were here, I would tell you what an inspiration you are to me. **I miss you**, Tía. I know I'll always miss you and that's okay. It will be an extra part of me that will make me stronger and kinder.

HOPE
Chapter 10

The following week, kids from my current events class continued to promote our cause by collecting donations and posting positive signs, like "I Stand with Immigrants" and "Families Belong Together" at school and at Riverfront Community Center. On top of that, Makena and Evette had both texted me that our World by Us page was still receiving a bunch of likes and follows. It was proof that we had truly opened hearts.

On Wednesday, we had just finished soccer practice when the coach called Ainsley, Violeta, and me into her office. Turns out, all three of us had been selected by both the DC Premiere and Elite Athletica clubs! It was up to us to choose who we would play for. After a silly victory dance in the coach's office, Violeta headed straight home to watch her nieces while her mom and aunt went to work. I texted Sierra and we made plans to celebrate with Violeta later at our favorite ice cream shop.

The next day, in current events, Violeta wasn't there. Mr. Bernstein wanted to wait for her, but when she didn't show up after ten minutes, he started class by playing

BREAKING NEWS

MARITZA OCHOA FROM DC BILINGUAL

LIVE

my TV interview from the Soccer Showcase. When my interview came on, Sierra and Raheem led everyone in chanting, "Maritza's gonna defeat-cha." They must have learned that from Makena and Evie!

In the midst of the cheers, Violeta opened the classroom door and poked her head in.

"Violeta!" Mr. Bernstein beamed. She waved at everyone and then asked Mr. Bernstein to come out to the hallway. As Mr. Bernstein closed the door behind him, the whole class erupted into confused murmurs.

After a few minutes, the door opened and Mr. Bernstein was back at the front of the room with a huge smile on his face.

"There's someone who wants to meet all of you," he

said excitedly. Just then Violeta walked in with her uncle Andrés!

The entire class leaped to its feet and burst into cheers. A woman in a green dress followed them in. She smiled at our screams of surprise and delight.

When the class finally quieted, Mr. Moreno spoke.

"Gracias por todo. Thank you for everything," he said. "I'm forever grateful. When Ms. Cantu and Violeta told me that a bunch of kids worked so hard to help my family, I couldn't believe it. Face-to-face with you right now, I see hope. Thank you!"

Next thing I knew, everyone had jumped out of their seats and crowded around Mr. Moreno for handshakes and hugs. Violeta pulled me up to the front.

"Tío Andrés and Ms. Cantu, this is Maritza Ochoa. The one I told you about. She led all of this."

"Muchas gracias, Maritza," said Violeta's uncle. I felt my heart burst as he gave me a hug. The woman, Ms. Cantu, touched my arm.

"I've known your abuela for a long time," she smiled. "I was so moved by your words at the Soccer Showcase that I made a few calls on behalf of Mr. Moreno to secure his release."

That's when it dawned on me that Ms. Cantu was my

abuela's bigwig guest! She hugged me and quietly watched the class celebrate.

"So does this mean you'll get citizenship now?" Raheem asked Violeta's uncle.

"Not yet, but one step at a time," Mr. Moreno answered. "It's not over, but I get to go home."

Violeta put her arm around my shoulders. "You did it, Itza!"

"*We* did it!" I said. I soaked in the joyful voices, the fist bumps, high fives, and laughter. This is America when we lead with our hearts.

abuela, abuelo *(ah-BWEH-lah, ah-BWEH-loh)*—grandmother, grandfather

¡Ay, viejo! *(Eye, VYEH-hoh)*—Oh, old man!

baleadas *(bah-lay-AH-dahs)*—Honduran dish made with tortillas, beans, and cheese

ballet folklórico *(bah-LEY fohl-KLOH-reeh-coh)*—type of traditional Mexican dance

charro *(CHA-rroh)*—Mexican horseman

chicas *(CHEE-kahs)*—girls

claro *(CLAH-roh)*—of course

cotija *(coh-TEE-hah)*—Mexican cheese

elote *(eh-LOH-teh)*—Mexican grilled corn

elotes

familia *(fah-MEE-lyah)*—family

felicidades *(feh-lee-see-DAH-dehs)*—congratulations

fiesta *(FYEHS-tah)*—party

ganamos *(gah-NAH-mohs)*—we won

gracias *(GRAH-syahs)*—thank you

gracias a la vida *(GRAH-syahs ah lah VEE-dah)*—thank you to life

gracias por todo *(GRAH-syahs pohr TOH-doh)*—thank you for everything

hola *(OH-lah)*—hello

huaraches *(waw-RAH-chez)*—Mexican sandals

jarabe tapatío *(hah-RAH-beh tah-pah-TEE-oh)*—Mexican dance

La Bamba *(lah BAHM-bah)*—Mexican wedding dance

lo siento *(loh SYEHN-toh)*—I'm sorry

mi gente *(mee HEN-teh)*—my people

mija *(MEE-hah)*—dear girl

muchachas *(moo-CHAH-chahs)*—girls

muchachos *(moo-CHAH-chohs)*—boys

baleada

muchas gracias *(MOO-chahs GRAH-syahs)*—thank you very much

muy triste *(mwee TREES-teh)*—very sad

prima *(PREE-mah)*—cousin

pupusas *(poo-POO-sahs)*—grilled Salvadoran flatbread stuffed with beans, meat, and cheese

¡Qué feo! *(keh FEH-oh)*—How ugly!

¡Que golazo! *(keh go-LAH-zoh)*—What a goal!

salteñas *(sahl-TEH-nyas)*—Bolivian meat pie

¡Sí se puede! *(see seh PWEH-deh)*—Yes we can!

son buenísimos *(sohn bweh-NEE-see-mohs)*—are great

son jorocho *(sohn joh-ROH-choh)*—Mexican folk music

suerte *(SWEHR-teh)*—luck

Tajín *(tah-JEEN)*—spicy Mexican condiment

tía, tío *(TEE-ah, TEE-oh)*—aunt, uncle

¿Todo bien? *(TOH-doh BYEHN)*—All good?

tu lucha es mi lucha *(too LOO-chah es mee LOO-chah)*—your fight is my fight

vamos *(VAH-mohs)*—we go

zapateado *(zah-pah-teh-AH-doh)*—Mexican tap dance

CHANGEMAKERS

When Maritza decided to stand up and speak out for her friend Violeta, that spark to help one family turned into a rally that made hundreds of people see the problems immigrant families face, and want to help. As Maritza says, "We are young. No one expects us to be leaders, so we must expect it of ourselves." Check out these stories from real Latina activists who are doing important work to change their communities and change the world.

Daphne Frias, age 23

Daphne was born a fighter. She weighed a little over one pound when she was born, and she's lived with cerebral palsy all her life. As a child, she zoomed around in her walker or wheelchair and made her presence known—and heard!

Today, Daphne uses that fighting spirit to speak out for others. She uses the power of her voice to make room for people with disabilities to be part of the causes they care about. She's organized accessible transportation to take people to rallies and marches.

DAPHNE FRIAS

Along with Greta Thunburg and other climate activists, Daphne helped organize 2019's Climate Strike in NYC. She speaks out passionately about the importance of gun control and school safety. She says, "Just because you have a disability doesn't mean you can't be amazing!" When negative news or sad stories start to get her down, Daphne thinks about how she can spread light in the darkness. She says it doesn't have to be anything grand or public. Even just checking in with a friend to see how she is doing brings joy into the world. "Remember that you have the power to change things now," Daphne says. "You don't have to wait until you're an adult. All you need is your voice and your passion for making change."

Sophie Cruz, age 10

Sophie has been an activist since she was five years old. Although Sophie was born in the United States and is a US citizen, her parents are immigrants from Oaxaca, Mexico. They are undocumented, which means they don't have US citizenship and could be deported. On a visit to Washington, DC, five-year-old Sophie made it through security barricades

to meet Pope Francis. Sophie had a very important message to deliver. In her handwritten letter, she asked the pope to protect undocumented people like her parents. The next day, the pope brought up this issue with Congress, encouraging more openness and compassion for immigrants.

In 2017, when Sophie was six, she was invited back to Washington, DC, to speak at the Women's March. She began her speech with these words: "We are here together, making a chain of love to protect our families. Let us fight with love, faith, and courage so that our families will not be destroyed."

Today, Sophie continues to inspire people to open their hearts to immigrant families and to treat them with respect and compassion.

To learn more about speaking up for those who can't, read *Stand Up for Yourself & Others* and *A Smart Girl's Guide: Race & Inclusion*.